Teachers' Day

A Philosophical Drama in Three Acts

Rajeshwar Prasad

TSL Drama

First published in Great Britain in 2025
By TSL Publications, Rickmansworth

Copyright © 2025 Rajeshwar Prasad

ISBN: 978-1-917426-19-0

Cover courtesy of :
https://pixabay.com/illustrations/board-think-structure-solution-752051/

Teachers' Day

There is an international seminar on 'Man and Divinity' sponsored by the Higher Education Ministry of the Central Government on Teachers' Day. Several college and university teachers are participating in the seminar. It is a big lecture hall connected to a standard library full of higher-level books. Two participants MAX and KIM, two college professors, are sitting during the special session 'one to one'. While waiting for KNOW ALL, the chief guest who has won the 'Novel Prize' and 'World's Best Teacher Award', they are discussing different issues related to man, knowledge, wisdom, the world, life, and God.

MAX, who has a Doctorate of Philosophy on 'Man and Divinity', feels proud showing his wisdom and knowledge on such topics.

KIM believes there is no difference between an illiterate man and a literate man. There is no meaning of wisdom and knowledge in the life of man. All types of knowledge are meaningless. The life of man is absurd.

They continue discussing and at last, the director DAR announces that KNOW ALL will not be attending as the plane he was on has crashed with all lives lost.

The seminar is postponed until further notice. They will be informed of the new date through the proper channel.

Running Time

65 minutes

Characters

MAX   45 years old, college teacher from Griefland

KIM   40 years old, college teacher from Lightland

DAR   55 years old, director of the seminar.

Set

A conference room with large tables to allow people to talk.

Flower pots, books, chairs, tables, diaries, pens, loudspeakers, flashboards, and a stage. Projector and blackboards.

Some participants roam hither and thither.

Act 1

Lights up.

An announcement is heard. "Registered participants, attention, please! Chief Guest KNOW ALL will arrive at 1:00 p.m. Please take your allocated seat as indicated on the board for your table number. Discussants will address the topic allocated."

A flashboard with the words:

TEACHERS' DAY – 5 SEPT 2018

'MAN AND DIVINITY'

TABLE NUMBER: 17

PARTICIPANTS' NAMES: MAX AND KIM

MAX: [*Books, a diary, and a pen on the table.*] Happy Teachers' Day!

KIM: [*Books, a diary, and a pen on the table.*] Thanks a lot, and same to you!

MAX: Knowledge commands the world.

KIM: [*Silent.*]

MAX: How beautiful and happy is the day for us today!

KIM: [*Silent.*]

MAX: [*Shows Roman alphabet.*] The world moves around only twenty-six letters.

KIM: Which twenty-six letters?

MAX: All know.

KIM: I'm confused.

MAX: The world is wide and large, but moves around only twenty-six Roman letters.

KIM: How?

MAX: All activities are defined by these letters – good and bad – and also life and death.

KIM: But my views are different.

MAX: What?

KIM: Twenty-six letters move around stupidity.

MAX: No...no. These letters are used by us when we need to reveal facts or things. This may be right or wrong.

KIM: What?

MAX: Really, an amazing invention!

KIM: What...what?

MAX: Very mysterious.

KIM: I know that the command of these twenty-six letters is absurd and imprisons him in the black hall to suffer and weep for ever. The world is a dream.

MAX: The world is not a dream but rather full of beauty and we are always in its clutch.

KIM: No...no.

MAX: You must feel the glory and beauty of the world and its making. The humans who arrive here never want to go back from this beautiful and magical world. You can understand its beauty and significance.

KIM: You don't know. Man is the slave of worldly beauty which is quite false.

MAX: I know the command and magic of these letters – I know the beauty and pleasure of the world, but you do not.

KIM: All that is an illusion that fades away quickly.

MAX: Try to know and understand! Everything is under the command of wisdom and knowledge.

KIM: Knowledge is meaningless in this dry land.

MAX: Wisdom and knowledge can make the world fertile.

KIM: The world can't be fertile in any condition. This is the sorrow-land.

MAX: [Boldly.] Every work and activity is undertaken according to these letters, but man uses these letters according to his practice.

KIM: Yes, but.

MAX: What?

KIM: Alphabets can compose many good words and ideas, but cannot change the absurdity of the world. Man uses these letters, but its end is the same – the same as all other things of the world.

MAX: No.

KIM: Why not?

MAX: [*Convincing tone.*] The knowledge of man can turn anything in its own way. It depends on a man and his knowledge.

KIM: I know that.

MAX: [*Seriously. Pointing the index finger of his right hand.*] If you know it, why do you not accept my findings?

KIM: Know. I accept it differently.

MAX: What?

KIM: [*Looking directly at* MAX.] I know that man uses knowledge in his own ways. But the end is the same. The final result is the same for all.

MAX: No.

KIM: Why not?

MAX: The end of anything is according to knowledge.

KIM: My ideas are quite different.

MAX: [*Nodding.*] What?

KIM: The end of anything is according to the law of Nature.

MAX: The same thing is used differently. It depends on the knowledge of man. Differently! It depends on his approach – whether it is creative or destructive.

KIM: I agree but the result of any deed is the same. That is an absurdity over time.

MAX: [*Frankly.*] The end of anything is as one needs and practices in life.

KIM: You are right but the use of knowledge is limited. [*Shows some images and short videos of laughing and weeping men and women.*]

MAX: Yes. I know.

KIM: Once, our knowledge fails, we embrace that which is a natural and eternal fact. [*Continues to plays some videos of joy and sorrow and Tells MAX to watch them.*]

MAX: I agree with that point.

KIM: But this is not the last. The fact is that by using knowledge one can't ignore the natural fact. We all can pass our life in reason. But finally, we all embrace that which is an eternal fact. [*Shows videos and photographs of several tragedies, accidents, deaths, engraving and cremation.*]

MAX: By using the knowledge we can do the work which remains undone till now.

KIM: No.

MAX: If there is no use of knowledge how are we to change the fates of different students? I alone have changed the fate of thousands of students in my time as a teacher. [*Shows some videos and photographs of some of his successful students in his teaching career.*]

KIM: [*Laughs.*] Ha...ha!

MAX: Why?

KIM: You are just like a little boy.

MAX: Please don't use such language here. We are sitting in a seminar and other teachers are looking at us.

KIM: No matter. All know that we are minors. All know that our work is always childish. We are children and ours is childish. We all are as ignorant armies deputed on duty. But what happens next, we don't know. [*Smiles.*]

MAX: Why do you say such things among others?

KIM: All this is common. This is not a matter of shame.

MAX: This is not a matter.

KIM: [*Confidently.*] This is the only matter and we all are children – our knowledge is childish. We use our knowledge to save a dying person or to escape earthquakes and volcanoes, but at some point our knowledge is shattered and our attempts become meaningless.

MAX: [*Pause.*] What?

KIM: Knowledge is meaningless. In the course of time, all this is meaningless. The same knowledge becomes meaningless.

MAX: [*Very seriously showing the kits and pamphlets given to them by the seminar organisers related to 'Man and Divinity'.*] We are teachers and we are here at a seminar to discuss 'Man and Divinity'. If we talk in this way, no fruitful outcome will take place and our discussion will end in a fuss.

KIM: [*Laughs.*] Ha...ha...ha...There is nothing fruitful in this world. The world is a fuss. We all go to the same unknown homes after death.

MAX: Knowledge is always fruitful. Ignorance is harmful.

KIM: No. The meaning of both things is the same.

MAX: [*Confidently.*] It's only because of our knowledge that we are working in senior posts in the Department of Education and we get a handsome salary. This post and its handsome salary distinguish us as men of knowledge and wisdom. This is why we are different, the identity of a coolie is different. We all are different.

KIM: You have only absurd ideas. We are all the same.

MAX: We have meaningful ideas. We know and can therefore change the world.

KIM: None can change the world and its systems.

MAX: Knowledge can.

KIM: Why do you not understand the facts? Knowledge is as meaningless as any other thing in the world.

MAX: Knowledge is the main weapon that separates man from every other being of the world.

KIM: Man is naturally separated. He need not be separated.

MAX: How?

KIM: This world is for all beings, except man.

MAX: You say. Is a man alien?

KIM: Yes.

MAX: How?

KIM: Man is alien so he needs the degrees of worldly education, while all other beings have no degrees and live naturally.

MAX: This degree of institution qualifies a man as man, otherwise man is also like an animal.

KIM: No.

MAX: Why?

KIM: Man's degree is quite absurd and his degree is as useless as a dry leaf separated from trees.

MAX: For a teacher you are talking as a rustic.

[*Shows photographs delivering lectures in classrooms.*]

KIM: We all are rustics.

MAX: Villagers are rustic. We are highly qualified.

[*Shows several certificates.*]

KIM: No...no.

MAX: I am right.

KIM: We are the same. There is no difference.

MAX: Why not?

KIM: The same is the condition of all – either we are educated or uneducated.

MAX: No.

KIM: Why not? We are the same...the same.

[*An announcement is heard. "KNOW ALL will arrive at 1*

p.m. The seminar is going well. Happy Teachers' Day!"]

MAX: [*Seriously. Showing his medals.*] Sorry. Are you a folk man? Why are you talking like an illiterate? You are a college teacher and your output should be like a teacher. You are a very responsible person and it should be always in your mind.

KIM: [*Frankly and seriously. Showing some pictures of tragic death of teachers.*] I do know and understand all this. But man can never depart from the state which is naturally inherited.

MAX: [*Strongly.*] You talk like an uncultured man. It seems that you are out of this world.

KIM: You must know we are all uncultured folk. We're not teachers. None is educated. We all have the same condition after death. We all are awarded the same size place after death in the lowly bed. Then there is no difference between a degree holder and labourer. All become the same once again. Five elements into five elements! So, our knowledge is also absurd.

MAX: No.

KIM: I say fact.

MAX: No, you are wrong.

KIM: No knowledge can remove man from death. Look at these photographs. One day, we all naturally go to that place. [*Shows several photographs of dead kings and queens.*]

MAX: Knowledge saves the lives of millions each year.

KIM: How?

MAX: When one falls ill, he is treated by the knowledge of medical science. That is the knowledge that saves man.

KIM: But for how much time?

MAX: Till his old age.

KIM: It may be. But he is not saved forever. At some stage the use of man's knowledge fails and he becomes the same as all others.

MAX: This is the reason behind us.

[*An announcement is heard. "KNOW ALL will arrive at 1 p.m. The seminar is going well. Happy Teachers' Day!"*]

KIM: [*Long pause.*] 'Man and Divinity' is the topic for today's discussion. No doubt man has developed his knowledge. But he has not changed natural eternity. Man is the same and will remain the same.

MAX: Man has done many works as a result of knowledge gained. He has reached the moon and Mars. He is trying to make his dwelling place there. This has become possible only because of science and knowledge.

KIM: [*He shows videos of scientists' achievements.*] Man has gained much knowledge, but he has not changed the mortal state of man. He is in the same condition as he was in the past.

MAX: In the past, man did not go to the moon. Now we easily go there.

KIM: But despite all this, our knowledge is limited and till now we have failed to change the state of the absurdity of life.

MAX: [*Long pause.*] Have you submitted your paper?

KIM: No.

MAX: Why?

KIM: I have no new paper on any topic.

MAX: No paper?

KIM: Yes.

MAX: How will you get a certificate of participation?

KIM: I don't need a certificate.

MAX: Why have you come here?

KIM: Unintentionally, I got an invitation.

MAX: I got an invitation through the proper channel.

KIM: [*Laughs.*] Ha...ha.

MAX: Why do you laugh?

KIM: [*Surprisingly.*] I think that's how little knowledge you have! You are really a child.

MAX: [*Happily, proudly.*] Please let me say that I am not a man of little knowledge. I have a PhD degree in 'Man and Divinity' from the University of Divinity, Mysticland. I am an expert and have attended several seminars and delivered long lectures on such topics. I have full knowledge of Theology.

[*Shows KIM a certificate.*]

KIM: [*Laughing.*] But. You are indeed a child. You don't know we all move to death through the proper channels of expectations.

MAX: I have specialized. I have done many courses on it.

KIM: But all knowledge is meaningless. Your life is also meaningless, like all others who are illiterate.

MAX: Do you not feel the difference between literate and illiterate people?

KIM: I feel no difference.

MAX: Why?

KIM: Because there is no difference in the eyes of death, which makes our life absurd.

MAX: Do you not feel a difference between you and a peon in your college?

KIM: Of course! No difference.

MAX: Are you fit mentally?

KIM: I am like all others in this world. We are all ill. We are suffering. We all die and our life is absurd – either we are holding high degrees or not, either we are working in high posts or we are coolies.

[*Shows several photographs of suffering and death.*]

MAX: Really, you are out of the world. Your talk is quite nonsense.

KIM: All are the same. I know my talk is nonsense for you. I know your talk is also nonsense.

MAX: Dear professor, know! I am an expert. I am a specialist in such fields. I know what is not known by others. Know. I am a theologian and we are in touch with God.

KIM: It is a hundred percent false. It is a lie.

MAX: Sorry. You are a man of stupidity! How have you become a professor? Oh! Shame...shame.

KIM: [*Smiling.*] You don't know anything about the world. I know. The fact is that you are an expert on nonsense. The subject to which you are an expert is not. There is no God. There is no theology. If there is no theology, you are an expert on which things? If there is no life how can you say that you have a life? Really, the life you have is quite false. It is a lie and disappears like a bubble of water. It fades away within a moment before eyes, and man continues to see helplessly. And after it there is no life – there is no need for theology.

MAX: That is a theology that shows light to all.

KIM: Heh! There is no theology. There is no God.

MAX: Then?

KIM: That is Nature-logy which commands us and shows us a light that we all are aliens and our life is absurd.

MAX: You are far removed from the facts. You should learn to understand the meaning of man, life, and divinity.

KIM: Whatever you are talking about, a man and the world, but that is absolutely false and absurd. So, all the knowledge related to all this is meaningless.

MAX: You are false. We have other facts and facets of life. If we ignore all this, we go away from the root. The fact is that life is meaningful. There is the realm of God. The life of man is joyful and is better than life in heaven.

KIM: You have only stupid ideas.

MAX: You do not know this, so you say what you do.

KIM: You live in a state of illusion.

MAX: I understand the reason behind the sense of isolation and alienation is because of global changes.

KIM: No.

MAX: What?

KIM: This type of sense is inherited not because of global change.

MAX: You are out of the way.

Both leave their chairs and go to the cloakroom.

Lights down.

Act 2

Lights up.

An announcement is heard. "KNOW ALL will arrive at 1 p.m. The seminar is going well. Happy Teachers' Day!"

MAX and KIM take their seats.

KIM: No I am only on the way.

MAX: How?

KIM: [*Philosophically and seriously.*] The world is ignorant that all die but they do not accept their non-existence and finally they die. They all see dying and departing from here proving their life meaningless but they do not think about all this and continue to live absurdly. It is a mystery that they all become prey to: time and fate.

MAX: This is a cycle of Nature, not ignorance.

KIM: No. This is the ignorance of man.

MAX: All say all this absurdly.

KIM: This is only meaningful otherwise everything is absurd. Life is absurd. The world is absurd.

MAX: Your ideas are absurd.

KIM: My ideas are meaningful. The life of man in the world is absurd.

MAX: No.

KIM: Believe. Your knowledge will fail one day and you will embrace the absurdity.

MAX: Know professor, I have changed the fates of millions in education centres. I have founded a dozen institutions in fully backward areas and thousands of students get an education. They would be illiterate if I had not done so. In my every walk of life, I have established records which you can see and understand. Wherever I go I gain respect and honour. All love me. All respect me. My situation is quite different – which you can't imagine. Most participants are known in this seminar too. I know them well. They know me well. They are aware of my scholarly knowledge.

[*Shows photographs and videos of institutions.*]

KIM: [*Laughs.*] Ha...ha! Absurd ideas...

MAX: Stupid words!

KIM: [*Shows various videos and photographs to* MAX.] All works for others or self will be in vain in the course of time. The fact is that none respect you. There is no student produced in education centres who knows the way to be free from the powerful clutch of death; death which is the most powerful agency of the cosmos. All fail to control it until now. Your knowledge is tiny and useless in this regard. Have you the knowledge to command time? Away from the command of Death?

MAX: Do you know my disciples? Thousands of thousands all over the world!

KIM: Know! There is no disciple of anyone. Rather they are under the clutch of lust and greed which is also false and is shattered before the tide of death.

MAX: [*Gazing seriously at him.*] I am unlike you. I have done much work for others. So, they all regard me. They all love me.

KIM: None respects you. None loves you. You live in a state of illusion. You are a fool.

MAX: You are a conservative man which is why you don't serve others. There is none with you.

KIM: No. Know! The whole world is conservative. We all are conservatives.

MAX: No.

KIM: [*Lightly pushes* MAX's *body for a moment.*] Ha...ha! Know! How conservative the world is! It very easily helps us depart for our home. It always tries to send us back home. It has no regard for us. It is merciless. The world has only one thing which is a tribute.

MAX: Except this, do you expect anything?

KIM: The tribute is meaningless. No tribute awakens the man in the grave. No tribute makes man alive. No tribute gives fire to a man in the grave.

MAX: [*Silent.*]

KIM: Do you understand all this?

MAX: I do.

KIM: This is not enough. This is not the end of my findings.

MAX: [*Silent.*]

KIM: Tears which are produced by kith and kin are false. None goes to the grave with the man.

MAX: Whatsoever. But we have to live. We have to do for life in any condition.

KIM: [*Shocked.*] We have to do nothing for life because it is quite meaning-less. It is quite false. It is a cheater. It has created all of us. We do everything for it. But despite all this, it cheats on us. It gives us no memory of where our home is. [*Tears.*]

MAX: [*Sadly.*] What happened to you?

KIM: [*Sadly.*] Nothing.

MAX: [*Pause. Sadly.*] But tears from your eyes.

KIM: I have missed my home. I don't know my original home. We all live in others' homes. My condition is worse than an animal's.

MAX: Really, death is not avoidable. So, a man should learn to live here happily.

KIM: Now you don't understand the world and its people. It shows that the world has no life so we always try to compromise with this absurd state of man and we all do it happily, forgetting the absurdity of life.

MAX: [*Silent. Looks sad.*]

KIM: None can win over this powerful agency. None knows to

maintain life on this earth.

MAX: Whatsoever. But we must live happily and consider that this is heaven. I also like to say that really the world is heaven and the best place in the cosmos.

KIM: This is not a matter. None can live here happily, because this world is a tears-land. This world is a fake-land. The real land is unseen and unknown.

MAX: [*Long pause. Showing scriptures.*] Have you read these scriptures?

KIM: Which scriptures?

MAX: Religious texts?

KIM: [*Eagerly.*] Yes...yes.

MAX: Regularly?

KIM: Yes...yes.

MAX: At least ten times?

KIM: Thousands of times!

MAX: Thousands of times?

KIM: Yes...yes, professor.

MAX: Of other religions too?

KIM: Yes...all...all! Every scripture, but all in vain.

MAX: Despite all this, you don't know the world, man, and life?

KIM: I know well.

MAX: What do you find there?

KIM: Quite false ideas! They are absolutely false.

MAX: False ideas?

KIM: Absolutely!

[*An announcement is heard. "KNOW ALL will arrive at 1 p.m. The seminar is going well. Happy Teachers' Day!"*]

MAX: None in the world can ill-fame the scripture. None says that scriptures are absurd. They are our mirrors. They show our path to God. They are the sciences of God and were written by God to follow the path of truth so that one can live in this world happily following virtues. It teaches us what is right and what is wrong. Whoever has missed following the right path reaches hell.

KIM: You are quite ignorant.

MAX: How?

KIM: You don't know the world.

MAX: I know well. I have read it very deeply.

KIM: [*Laughs.*] Ha...ha!

MAX: [*Agitated. Angrily.*] Foolish men always laugh.

KIM: Do you see me as a fool?

MAX: No.

KIM: But.

MAX: [*Silent.*]

KIM: [*Frankly.*] This is a fact. All is meaningless.

MAX: [*Silent.*]

KIM: There is no text which shows where my home is and when I will return to my home. All are vague. They are on life, death, fate, body, soul, world, deeds, sin, virtue, God, heaven, hell, and salvation, but no scripture on our home.

MAX: Is it not our home?

KIM: No. I have to go back to my home but that is quite known though I always try to know. But all in vain.

MAX: [*Amazed.*] Is this not home?

KIM: No.

MAX: Why are you living here?

KIM: I am passing some time here. This is a station of my long journey and when it is finished it will also be forgotten.

MAX: [*Silent.*]

KIM: The world which you see is false. The home which you see is of others'.

MAX: But.

KIM: We are aliens and we all return from here leaving everything.

MAX: I wish you would change your mindset.

KIM: I needn't change, because I am right.

MAX: The world in which we live is very wide and large. Different types of ideas come from time to time and all this is expressed by them. But all is not real. When people are isolated, they have such feelings and we all embrace such ideas from time to time.

KIM: You are blurring.

MAX: No. Know. Life is the name of all this.

KIM: I needn't know because I am absolutely right.

KIM: This is not a matter in which to be right or to be wrong, rather learn to live happily and remain away from such senses of despair and isolation. Life has been given by God and we must enjoy it as happily as we can.

KIM: In every deed of man loss is hidden – in every walk of life woe is hidden. The gain and pleasure which we see are entirely momentary.

MAX: Do you know of mine?

KIM: Nothing is to you to be known.

MAX: Know and feel how happy my life is.

KIM: [Laughs.] Ha...ha!

MAX: Know. Whenever I move in the streets of my home town, several people come and pay their respects to me. Some have been taught by me. I have also taught their children and later their grandchildren.

KIM: [He jokes. Laughs loudly.] But all this has no meaning in life. You must know, ignorant boy.

MAX: [Stands up angrily. Speaks loudly.] Control yourself. Am I a boy? Do you not know me?

KIM: Sorry...I'm too sorry.

MAX: [Normal voice.] Only because of my deeds, do I live

happily. My wife is over-pleased when she sees such respect for me in the city.

KIM: My findings are indeed different. Whenever and wherever I go, all hate me. Even a dog of mine is not that pays respect to me.

MAX: It means to say that you are meaner than a dog.

KIM: No...no.

MAX: What do you mean to say?

KIM: It is not a matter to be meaner or greater, but rather a matter of existence.

MAX: What?

KIM: A matter of existence.

MAX: Where?

KIM: In this Griefland.

MAX: Are you an escapist?

KIM: No. I am a known person to life and the world.

MAX: I do not understand your ideas.

KIM: It is not easy to understand. So most people misunderstand and reach graves.

MAX: What do you like to say?

KIM: This is the matter of the existence of man in the world.

MAX: But why do you talk about a dog?

KIM: The dog lives at home, but I have no existence in the world. So, the dog shows ego and pride. It sometimes shows disrespect. It always tries to possess me. Whenever I give it something to eat, the dog comes and follows me and later forgets – and if there is a long gap, it begins to bite.

MAX: Man has no existence?

KIM: No existence. None has existed in this world except beasts. But who lives in the lap of Nature, accepts man's existence.

MAX: I have existence and I do exist and live in my home on my own accord.

KIM: You also have no existence.

MAX: Why do you always misinterpret everything?

KIM: Believe.

MAX: How can I believe it? You are quite out of tune with the world.

KIM: This is not a real matter.

MAX: Why not?

KIM: I am right. I know this is not our home and we have lived in others' homes for a short time. I wait to return to my home after death, but that is unknown to me. When, where and how?

MAX: But I never anticipate.

KIM: [*Shows a diary with his address.*] I always anticipate. My wife always suggests I remain alert for pickpockets, robbers, and vehicles.

MAX: All this is common.

KIM: Know something more.

MAX: What?

KIM: I always mention my location in my diary which I keep in my pocket wherever and whenever I go out.

MAX: [*Amazed.*] Why? Why?

KIM: My wife says to do so, because if any unpleasant event occurs, the police can take me or my dead body to my home. [*Shows a diary that mentions his address.*]

MAX: [*Long pause.*]

KIM: [*Pushes MAX slightly.*] Do you?

MAX: [*Pause.*] It seems that your life is in hell.

KIM: How?

MAX: [*Shows a picture of hell.*] You can imagine your condition. Even a dog is not at your command. Even you cannot win the heart of a dog.

KIM: That is not a matter.

MAX: [*Silent.*]

KIM: This shows the difference between man and other beings.

MAX: [*Silent.*]

KIM: How helpless a man is! Oh! Blood begins to come. Tears begin to come from me. Oh, all are bleeding here! Why Nature has brought it here! Only to weep and bleed!

[Weeps to see the state of man. Shows several photographs of men suffering weeping and dying.

An announcement is heard. "KNOW ALL will arrive at 1 p.m. The seminar is going well. Happy Teachers' Day!"

MAX: [*Sadly.*] Oh!

KIM: Oh! Only woes and sorrows all over the world. Bloodshed, violence, fever, fret, cancer, leprosy, etc. with our birth. Evil and disease are not in the world. All in the house of others.

MAX: [*Silent.*]

KIM: Aha! I wish I were also in my home here like all other beings. If it were, I would be very happy, like them.

MAX: Are animals and birds happier than men?

KIM: Undoubtedly!

MAX: [*Pause.*]

KIM: Undoubtedly!

MAX: How?

KIM: See and consider. Know! They live in their own home. The world is their home so they are happy. We have no home so we are not happy.

MAX: What?

KIM: They have no management but are happy. They have no store, no degree, no systems developed like us, and no constitution made by them. They never lose their eyesight till death. They sing the same song since creation and they take the same food.

MAX: Man?

KIM: Man always changes his language, food, and garments according to his one-time action only in search of existence.

MAX: [*Silent.*]

KIM: Think, Max. Think. Open the door of your mind and come to the ground of reality. You will find how a man's life is absurd.

MAX: Beasts also die like us.

KIM: But they never propose, rather we propose and they dispose. [*Shows a video in which he is trying to tempt a pigeon to eat mustard seeds, but in vain.*]

MAX: [*Silent.*]

KIM: Think! They never come to man to be our friend. A man goes to them because man is always in search of existence.

MAX: [*Long pause.*] I am shocked at your attitude.

KIM: Why?

MAX: How misfortunate you are!

KIM: You are also in the same condition.

MAX: No.

KIM: This is a fact.

MAX: No...no.

KIM: [*Looking directly at* MAX.] Know, the professor of divinity! I always remain shocked to see such an attitude of man; how he lives in the home of others!

MAX: Oh! Oh!

KIM: What happened to you Max?

MAX: [*Sadly.*] On this good day, you are also bleeding and tears are coming from your eyes.

KIM: Naturally.

MAX: [*Pause.*] Today the country is celebrating Teachers' day. All are glorifying one crore teachers in the country. One crore and thirty thousand people in the country are paying their respects to us.

KIM: I know.

MAX: Then why do you think such about the condition of man?

KIM: Naturally, such ideas come to me.

MAX: [*Silent.*]

KIM: [*Weeps. Tears flowing.*] My condition is miserable. I have to go home, leave everything and everyone.

MAX: Don't weep.

[*Pacifies.*]

KIM: [*Silent.*]

MAX: You are really misfortunate. Now you are in this state. Today the world is paying its respect to us and our knowledge which has shaped the future of thousands of students.

KIM: But their respect can't hold us here even for a moment when death occurs and makes life absurd.

MAX: We should forget such ideas.

KIM: I try to forget but the sense of fear, suspense, insecurity isolation, and loneliness are ever present.

MAX: Forget all this. Listen to me.

KIM: [*Silent.*]

MAX: Think a little. Only we are here who teach students and make them civilized. We bring different people to the path of a happy life otherwise they would have been like animals.

KIM: It would be far better if we were animals. We would have our home and we would be happy like them.

MAX: [*Amazingly.*] What are you telling me? How you are Kim!

KIM: Like you.

MAX: I am also like you?

KIM: Yes...yes. But my findings are different.

MAX: I show mercy to you because of your miserable state.

KIM: Your condition is the same.

MAX: No.

KIM: Think deeply. Look into your family history. History repeats itself. You will replace them. Let the time come.

MAX: I live in the present.

KIM: In this way, you can't ignore death.

MAX: But I don't think about the future.

KIM: I weep for the miserable condition of man in the world. [*Weeps.*]

MAX: I understand the reason behind your tears and fears. Actually, the world has changed. People are changed.

KIM: But fate has not changed.

MAX: [*Silent.*]

KIM: The same condition.

MAX: In the past, all were happy and lived happily together. Now we run behind material gain, so we move far away from values and virtues. Its outcome is that in every walk of life, we all are compelled to suffer.

KIM: Man has come here only to suffer.

MAX: No.

KIM: [*Frankly.*] I am right.

MAX: The real matter is that now there are global changes and their outcome is that man has become a machine. The condition is worse in developed countries. These are the reasons you suffer.

KIM: [*Silent. Sad.*]

MAX: But don't worry. Time changes. Everything changes. You must learn to change. God will help you. God will bless you.

KIM: No...no.

MAX: Why not?

KIM: There is no God.

MAX: [*Amazingly. Shows some images of the religious sites.*] Do you not believe in God?

KIM: That is not a matter of belief.

MAX: Do you believe in Him or not?

KIM: [*Frankly.*] Never.

MAX: This is the main reason for your sense of isolation and suffering. We all believe in Him and are very happy.

KIM: No...no.

MAX: Why not?

KIM: All are isolated and separated. There are different reasons – the reasons of caste, colour, community, creed, culture, country, race, sect, religion, etc.

MAX: But.

KIM: There are some reasons to delay going home. But there is no change in existence. All are alone here. You are also isolated. [*Shows a video of the sunrise and the sunset.*]

MAX: No. My situation is different.

KIM: You are also the same.

MAX: You must learn to accept others' findings.

[*Announcement: "All respected participants, attention, please! KNOW ALL will arrive at 1 p.m. Please make your way to the cafeteria for snacks and coffees within ten minutes and thereafter continue your fruitful discussions. Happy Teachers' Day!"*]

Lights down.

Act 3

Lights up.

Announcement: "Respected participants, attention, please! KNOW ALL will arrive at 1 p.m. Please return, take your seats and continue your fruitful discussions. Happy Teachers' Day!"

MAX and KIM return from the cafeteria and take their seats. Continue discussing.

KIM: [*Seriously.*] Do you feel that I am a rebel?

MAX: No.

KIM: Then?

MAX: Because you always talk differently.

KIM: That is not a matter.

MAX: But.

KIM: Natural interpretation.

MAX: There must be some practical ideas.

KIM: I also accept practical ideas.

MAX: But I always see you being different.

KIM: [*Shows a video of a dying person.*] This is natural. Whoever comes here accepts others' findings and passes time till it's his time to return to his home. This period of exile is very boring. So, all go from here.

MAX: Pass some hours here. In the evening you have to return home like all the others.

KIM: Yes.

MAX: Very good.

KIM: I am here to expect something good so I am interested to live here. But I always think about going home and about the way by which I will easily reach my home.

MAX: All are in a hurry to go but their works detain them.

KIM: All this is the reason for the world.

MAX: Yes.

KIM: The world is a reason.

MAX: None detains without a proper reason.

RAJ: But the reason is also meaningless.

MAX: Some works are meaningful.

KIM: No. Nothing is meaningful in the world.

MAX: My findings are different.

KIM: What?

MAX: Bad works and good works. Some which we like and some which we dislike! Some works are useful and others are harmful.

KIM: All are the same because all go in vain after death.

MAX: No.

KIM: Know. Go to graves and see the condition of man.

MAX: Here your ideas are alluring.

KIM: I am quite on the way.

MAX: You are not to the point and you want to blur the facts.

KIM: No. I am accurate to the point.

MAX: If everything is the same, why doesn't man do all the work equally? All are different.

KIM: Man is an illusion.

MAX: [*Silent.*]

KIM: [*Philosophically, seriously. Shows two videos of dying men – one of a king, the other of a beggar.*] Death is the most impartial agency which makes all men equal in the grave. The same! Either rich or poor! Whatever we are but the same treatment!

MAX: Understand the difference between fire and water.

KIM   There is no difference. Temporarily there is loss or benefit but later all are the same. After some time either we lose in fire or water. But we have loss and loss.

MAX: The world is not as you think. You must learn to argue meaningful points.

KIM: There is nothing meaningful. All accept decay and finally, all are automatically lost. We try hard to hold our rights in different ways. But man's possession is lost within a moment.

MAX: [*Shows a video of government records.*] Nothing is lost. There is a system of every management and we manage all things as per our needs and for its security. There is registration of every property in the honours' name and we are safe and secure. So there is no chance of the loss of possession.

KIM: You are wrong. You don't discuss the main point. Know, the fact is different.

MAX: What?

KIM: After death, we have no possessions.

MAX: No.

KIM: How?

MAX: They are transferred into our loved ones' names.

KIM: Ha...ha!

MAX: This is not a matter for mocking. You can know. Whatever property you have is transferred into your name after the death of your loved ones.

KIM: [*Long pause. Shows a video of dead king whose palms were empty.*] I have no property. I don't know. I have no possessions. I always try to possess but my partners say that this is my property and I say that that is my property.

MAX: How can one capture the property in your name?

KIM: They are influential and powerful.

MAX: Why do you not ask the help of the police?

KIM: They do not help.

MAX: Why?

KIM   They say that it is a matter for the Land and Revenue Department.

MAX: Have you registered it in the offices of the government?

KIM: [*Silent.*]

MAX: Tell me.

KIM: After the death of my parents, I have visited the offices several times to register but some of my family members have filed objections and therefore the office has declared it a property of dispute.

MAX: The property of dispute?

KIM: Yes.

MAX: Have you appealed to the apex authority?

KIM: Yes.

MAX: What was its decision?

KIM: The decision is pending.

MAX: Why?

KIM: Because they are very busy doing other more important work than mine.

MAX: Other works?

KIM: Yes.

MAX: Which works?

KIM: [*Shows a video of the crowd on the court campus.*] There is a more important case to hear which is very sensitive. So, most of the judges are hearing such cases. My case is a matter of title suit, so it is not considered an urgent case.

MAX: You should pray to hear the case as soon as the court can.

KIM: I have prayed to them but in vain.

MAX: Do you have a counsel?

KIM: Yes, I have.

MAX: He should be active.

KIM: He is active and says to let the proper time come. Everything happens in time, not according to the will of man.

MAX: It means you have had no possession until now.

KIM: Really, no possession. I never tell a lie.

MAX: I suggest you make a request to the President, who will issue a guideline for the quick hearing of the case.

KIM: I have done all this.

MAX: What happened?

KIM: Nothing...nothing. He is the same.

MAX: No.

KIM: I have the same finding.

MAX: They will take action against guilty persons.

KIM: No...nothing.

MAX: Don't worry. Let the time come. The decision will be delivered in your favour automatically.

KIM: I know it.

MAX: Really, everything is commanded by time.

KIM: Whatsoever.

MAX: I pray to God to award justice to you.

KIM: Don't name God.

MAX: Why?

KIM: Such a word is very old. I am tired of listening to His name. I have listened to Him several times, but I have never seen Him.

MAX: It is very difficult to see or meet Him.

KIM: The things which have no existence cannot be seen.

MAX: God needs not be seen or questioned.

KIM: [Silent.]

MAX: What?

KIM: Very congested dwelling.

MAX: Very rush is life here.

KIM: Such types of problems are common in others' homes.

MAX: Do you live in a rented house?

KIM: Yes.

MAX: Why?

KIM: [Long pause.] Times have changed. Since the registration of property began, the land has become very costly so I live in a rented house.

MAX: Really, have you not your own home?

KIM: [Shows the address of his landlord.] Really? No. I never tell a lie.

MAX: But I have a palatial home in Lightland in which I live with my beautiful wife and two children.

KIM: Have you no grandchildren?

MAX: No, I have also grandchildren.

KIM: How many?

MAX: They are six.

KIM: It means to say that you are also a very busy person in the family.

MAX: Yes. I play with them. I pass time with them.

KIM: Are they peaceful?

MAX: They are quarrelsome.

KIM: Quarrelsome?

MAX: Yes.

KIM: Why do they quarrel?

KIM: For toys or toffees or sleeping or for eating.

KIM: Very serious matter this is!

MAX: No. This is a very simple matter.

KIM: Your family is in a very miserable condition. More dangerous than mine.

MAX: No problem.

KIM: You are surrounded by problems.

MAX: When they grow, their nature will be changed.

KIM: None will be changed. One by one all are victims.

MAX: This is not a serious matter.

KIM: This is a really serious matter and they will spoil your family.

MAX: No...no.

KIM: Now they quarrel for toys and in the future when they grow older, they will quarrel for property.

MAX: No...no.

KIM: You are trying to ignore the fact.

MAX: All do the same in childhood. But when they grow older, they are changed.

KIM: No. You are an illusion.

MAX: I have not seen such matters anywhere.

KIM: Know! Only because of this reason there are millions of cases in the courts.

MAX: And your children?

KIM: They are also very quarrelsome.

MAX: It means you will have also to face such complications.

KIM: No...no.

MAX: Why not?

KIM: I have no property. I earn and spend. I live in a rented house.

MAX: But it is no solution.

KIM: [*Smiling.*] No problem will come to me. The main reason for the dispute is property. I have no property. So I will have no such problems.

MAX: It may be...but.

KIM: [*Long pause.*] Don't think about all this.

MAX: Okay.

KIM: [*Pause.*] We have passed enough time. Perhaps, Know All will arrive soon. He will deliver his lecture for which we all are waiting impatiently.

MAX: Yes. I do hope.

KIM: Sometimes, I have a different feeling.

MAX: What?

KIM: I feel that he has not come and we will return home without listening to his lecture and guidelines.

MAX: He will surely come.

KIM: No. I have lost faith.

MAX: We should not lose faith.

KIM: But I am compelled to think all this.

[*An announcement is heard. "KNOW ALL will arrive soon. The seminar is going on successfully. Happy Teachers' Day!"*]

MAX: Aha! Aha! Listen...listen...to the announcement.

KIM: You are right. Okay. He is just about to arrive.

MAX: Yes...yes.

KIM: Of course.

MAX: Do you know him?

KIM: No.

MAX: No?

KIM: No.

MAX: Never?

KIM: Never. I have listened to his name only. I have also asked some others who told me that they have listened to his name but have never seen him.

MAX: Really, he is a great man! A man of knowledge and wisdom! A man of justice and equality! A man of values and virtues! World's Best Teacher Award Winner! The Nobel Prize Winner!

KIM: Have you seen him?

MAX: No.

KIM: How do you know him?

MAX: All say all this about him.

KIM: I think he is not as all think and know. Will he come here?

MAX: No...no. He is very sincere and punctual. All say that he reaches in time anywhere. His record is also satisfactory. His employer is also very satisfied with him.

KIM: But I don't believe that he will come today.

[*An announcement is heard. "KNOW ALL will arrive shortly. The seminar is going on successfully. Happy Teachers' Day!"*]

MAX: Aha! Listen to the announcement. He will arrive here within a few moments.

KIM: Okay.

MAX: Let's move to the central hall. [*Starts moving.*]

KIM: Very good.

[*Stands up and moves.*

An announcement is heard. "Unfortunately, we have lost communication with KNOW ALL. We do not know when he will arrive."]

MAX and KIM are sitting in the central hall.]

MAX: Listen to the announcement.

KIM: Listen. Oh! Oh!

MAX: What happened to him? May God save him!

KIM: What happened to him?

[*Director DAR arrives.*]

DAR: I have got important information. Please listen to me. Pray to God for Know All's happy arrival here. The signal system of his plane has failed. The door has been jammed. Now the plane is flying without any signal. It is not known in which direction his plane is going. The pilot told all passengers to evacuate with the help of parachutes to save their life before the plane crashes. They tried hard using their knowledge and wisdom to save their life but they all failed to unlock the door.

MAX: Oh...oh! Can we...?

KIM: Can your knowledge and wisdom of divinity call him here?

MAX: [*Silent.*]

KIM: If any?

MAX: Oh...no.

DAR: Oh! Oh! The most shocking information! The plane crashed. None is alive. He is no more. He has gone forever. [*Shows a video recording of the plane crash.*]

MAX: What about our seminar?

KIM: I wish him a happy home return!

DAR: The seminar is suspended till further information is available. You will all be informed through the proper channel as to when we will reconvene the seminar.

MAX: Oh! The seminar is postponed.

DAR: You are suggested to remain in contact with your employer. I wish you all a happy home return!

MAX: Sorry Teachers' Day!

[*In the meantime, a lyric entitled 'Man is alien...' is played and all leave the hall weeping.*]

Man is an alien, no joy
A man passes in ego, but a toy
Having a stream on the lip
To return home – to weep.
The world is a hope-land

Knowledge and wisdom
As fallen leaves or boredom –
All is meaningless here.
Life is absurd and woes bear.
The world is hope-land.

Lights down.